Orange Sparkles

Book 1 in the Magic Sparkles series

By Rachel Inbar

This book is dedicated to my children:

Hadas, Matan, Lilach, Abigail, Nomi and Yirmi

who seem to actually enjoy the ridiculous stories

I make up for them.

2 4 6 8 10 9 7 5 3 1

Published by Magic Sparkles Publishing

ISBN: 978-3-9519929-0-7

For permission requests, please email
rachelinbar@gmail.com

Contents

Chapter 1 - Exciting News

Sunday afternoon was movie afternoon. My little brother, Noah; my sister Elise and me, Megan, always watched a movie with my mom while my dad napped. It was practically a family tradition. As soon as we'd finish cleaning up after lunch, my mom would put the phones on silent, dim the lights, and pop the popcorn. Noah and I would somehow gravitate toward the living room, always seeming to get there just as my mom switched on the tv, fiddled with the remote control, and got everything ready.

Then, we'd plop down on the couch together—my mom always on the left, next to Elise, and Noah usually beside her. My mom was good at choosing movies—usually funny ones—and I didn't care what we were watching anyway, as long as there was enough popcorn.

That Sunday, my mom said we were going to skip the movie. I probably should have guessed that something was up, but instead I assumed she just didn't feel like it... It crossed my mind that the weather had just started to be warm enough to take a walk outside—maybe even down to the pond, to feed the ducks. There's something about throwing food to ducks and seeing them all crowd around to grab for it that I love. Noah and I often watch which duck gets the biggest piece and then one of us yells "winner!"

Once we finished cleaning up after lunch, I went to my room, flopped down on my bed and started messaging my best friend, Erin, about nothing in particular. A few minutes later, my parents called Noah and me to come to the living room. My dad was skipping his nap? They said they had some exciting news for us. I quickly typed in a 'brb'—be right back—to Erin and ran downstairs. *Finally!* I thought. *A puppy. They got us a puppy.* We'd been asking for one for so-so long. I'd promised to help take care of it and said I'd vacuum the sofa once a week—the carpet too, if I had to. It hadn't convinced my mom so far, but maybe now... That's what I was thinking, as I tumbled into the living room, nearly tripping on the navy-blue shag carpet, my eyes carefully scanning the room for the box where the puppy was hiding. Maybe if I listened carefully, I could at least hear some scratching noises. Noah came running too, nearly crashing into me.

"What?" we both said, breathless, at exactly the same moment. Then we looked at each other and cracked up. We were always saying things together. Noah's 3 years younger than I am. I'm 11 and he's 8, I have green eyes and long, reddish-brown hair that I usually wear in a ponytail. Noah has brown hair that's always too long, even right after a haircut, and bright blue eyes that everyone tells him are gorgeous. They are, but I would never tell him that. It's not part of the sister code. Trust me.

So far, my scanning hadn't revealed anything. I was beginning to worry that maybe I wasn't going to like their news so much—like maybe we were going to visit our parents' friends, Don and Lara, who always spend the whole time we're there talking to Mom and Dad and ignoring us. My Dad says guests shouldn't use devices, that it's impolite, but we have nothing else to do. Their baby, Cody, is either drooling over his toys, which I find totally disgusting, or asleep. It's not that I think it would be fun to play with him. I don't. But the stuff they talk about is always so boring. Don and Lara aren't big on snacks either. Lara might ask, in her snooty tone, "Would you like a cucumber or a pepper, dear?" It's like she's pretending to be British. I have no idea why my parents are friends with them. Also, there's nowhere to play, so we all sit in their den together. Any time Noah and I get too loud, our parents tell us to 'cool it', so we can't even have fun. We end up just kind of sitting there, twiddling our thumbs and counting down the minutes until we can leave. So... as long as it wasn't that we were going there...

Anyway, back to my puppy. No box. No suspicious scratching. Hmm. What could this mean? Maybe we were going to go to the pet store together and then I'd get to help pick out our little fur-ball. I'd choose the one that looked the most like me, with reddish-brown hair and green eyes. Can dogs actually have green eyes? I'd choose the one who looked like it would be the friendliest to walk. The kind my friends and neighbors would all want to pet when I took him out for a walk. One people wouldn't get mad at, even if he barked.

My sister, Elise, was in her special stroller next to the couch. Elise was born with Cerebral Palsy, which means her muscles don't work the way they should, because of something that's wrong in her brain. She's almost 4-and-a-half, but she can't walk or talk. Actually, she can't do much for herself—she even needs help eating. Elise does smile sometimes and she was smiling now, so maybe she knew something I didn't. Maybe they'd already let her pick out the dog. If so, it was probably going to be a fluffy, white poodle, which would be OK with me, although I'd prefer a Cocker Spaniel—with green eyes, of course.

My dad started to talk and I immediately understood that this wasn't going to be a new puppy or something like that. He looked super-serious and I sort of braced myself. "Since Elise was born," he began, sounding as if he'd rehearsed it, "we've made a lot of changes in our lives." Yup. We'd moved to a house where we could easily push her stroller. My mom had stopped working so she could take care of

Elise and take her to all sorts of therapy sessions. My dad had gotten a job with a lot more responsibility so that he could earn more money. He worked long hours and we saw him mostly on weekends and late at night—if we happened to be up way past our bedtimes. In the morning, he was gone before we woke up.

As usual, Noah was restless, jumping around and making a lot of noise, distracting everyone. My dad shushed him so he could continue talking.

"We're going to make another change soon—this time, a really big one." The others weren't big? Oh man! We were really in for something. "We're moving." Moving? That was all? OK. We'd moved before. It was actually kind of exciting. I remember unpacking my room last time. Mom was so proud of me for doing it all by myself, but actually, I was playing this game in my head where I was a poor orphan girl who had just been adopted and I was opening all the incredible boxes as if the things inside were magical. I put each item away carefully, like I imagined the orphan girl doing, hanging each dress on a hanger facing the same direction and handling every worn-out pair of sport socks as if it were precious. Then, since I felt like it was unfair that I had so much stuff, I prepared a bag of old things I didn't need any more and gave it to my mom. She went through it and kept some of the nicer clothes for Elise and donated the rest to charity.

After the move, I had been worried about making friends in my new school, but it was no big deal. There were lots of new kids and within a few days, I felt like I fit right in. It was hard even to remember the 'new kid' feeling, it had gone away so fast. We also hadn't moved that far—just to another suburb of Boston—so I could still meet up with my old friends sometimes. I still wished I could meet up with them more often, but I was sure we'd still go to summer camp together and maybe get together during school vacations. There's something about meeting new friends that make the old friends—except the ones who are really special—sort of fade away. Maybe I had faded away for them too...

I was thinking about all this, when from the corner of my ear I heard the word, "Israel". I know you can't say 'corner of my ear' but it makes me laugh every time I think about saying it, so I do. "Huh?" I managed to say, "Where?"

"Megan," my mom said impatiently. "You weren't listening. Dad said we're moving to Israel."

"Israel? Isn't Israel a country? Like in a different place, far away from here?" I was suddenly feeling sort of faint.

My mom looked worried. "It's going to be OK. I bet you'll get used to it in no time." she said.

"Yes." My dad continued. "We're moving to Israel, where I'm going to set up a research center for my company." Oh-My-Gosh. Israel? Wait. What did I know about Israel? OK. I quickly scanned my brain. I remembered seeing camels in one of my school books. "Are we going to have to get a camel instead of a car?" I asked. I was totally serious. My parents thought I was joking and my mom started laughing. "Um. They have cars there. It's a modern country." My dad opened his laptop and showed us a clip about Israel. There were kids picking fruit and big tall buildings, people surfing, restaurants, markets... You know, a normal kind of place. So many questions were going through my head that they seemed to be crashing into and trampling each other. I didn't think I'd remember all of them and I was pretty sure they all needed to be asked.

My thoughts screeched to a ridiculously loud stop and "When?" was the first thing that came out.

"In the summer." My mom said. Oh, no! We were going to be moving *really* far. Even farther than

Melissa, who had moved to Chicago. Noah looked at me, as if to see how I felt about all this before deciding how he felt. I was completely confused. I don't think I could have been more confused if they'd just told me we were moving to the moon.

"The su-summer?" I stammered. "We can't! I'm going to summer camp with my old friends!"

"I know that that was what we planned, Megan, but things have changed... I was offered a great job. Opening a research center is a huge promotion—and it so happens that there are some great clinical trials going on in Israel that might be able to help Elise." My dad explained.

I made a pouty face. I sort of liked excitement, but this was way too big of a change for me.

"And one more thing," my dad bit his lower lip. "You're going to have to learn Hebrew."

"What's Hebrew?" Noah wanted to know. Actually, I did too. The 'brew' part reminded me of coffee, but I guessed it didn't have much to do with that, since I didn't think we'd be working in a coffee shop there or anything. Maybe since it's a different country, they speak a different language?

"That's the language they speak in Israel." Ugh. I was right. Seriously? They don't speak English? I remembered my parents had watched a French movie once. It had writing on the bottom of the screen in English, and they had to read everything that was written there. It's not exactly like watching a movie, if you ask me. It's kind of like reading a movie and seeing some of the pictures that go along with it at the same time. OK, it has the music and sound effects too, but I'd never be able to watch a movie that way. I wanted to ask if we really had to move there, but the answer was clear.

How do you learn a new language? I mean, I never learned any language. I was kind of born speaking English. OK, I know I wasn't born talking, but I never had to learn it. It was just there. No one had to explain to me what ordinary things meant. That was what Vocabulary lesson was for. "How are we going to learn it?" I wanted to know. I sounded skeptical; I could tell.

"We signed you up for Hebrew lessons. You're going to go twice a week from now until we move." My dad said. My first thought was "Oh, great." You know the sarcastic kind... but my second thought was that it might be interesting to learn a new language. I like challenges, so maybe this would be a cool kind of challenge. "Will Noah and I go together?" That would might make it better. "Yup." OK. Cool. I was trying to process all this new information. A class with Noah. At least I'd have someone to goof off with if I got bored. Who knows? It might even be fun; since we wouldn't be getting grades or anything. We wouldn't, right?

"How long will we live in Israel?" I asked my dad.

"Probably 2 years or so—it's hard to know." He said.

Was two years long enough for all of my friends to forget me? Or maybe they'd make new friends and wouldn't want to be my friends anymore when I got back. Thinking about this made my stomach hurt.

As I lay in my bed that night, wondering what it would be like to live in another part of the world, I drifted into thoughts of our new house, with our new puppy. I don't remember falling asleep, but I remember waking up in the morning and wondering if—or maybe even half-hoping—the whole thing had been a dream.

I ran downstairs too quickly and sort of tripped on the stairs, losing a shoe in the process. I ran back up to get it and then flew into the kitchen where my mom was quickly closing my lunchbox, probably to keep me from seeing the avocado sandwich she shoved in there. Try to explain to your mother that NO fourth grader eats avocado sandwiches. Really, it doesn't matter that I love avocado, there are some things I don't need my friends to know. On an ordinary day, I would have begged my mom to switch it, but all I was interested that morning was trying to get a better picture of what all this change was going to mean.

"Mom..." I started. "It's closed. That's what you're eating today." She was talking about my sandwich, so it *was* avocado...

"Whatever. That's not what I wanted to ask." My mom raised an eyebrow. I'm going to learn to do that when I grow up, really. It's such a cool trick.

"Shoot!" she said, meaning I should ask whatever I want.

"Where are we going to live? In Israel, I mean. Do they have regular houses?" I was more than a little worried. I hate bugs and there was no way I was going to live in some tent in the desert.

"Yeah, sure they have houses—they'll probably be a little different from what you're used to... Megan, this afternoon, you and Noah are going to have your first Hebrew lesson. I'll ask the teacher to show you more about Israel too." My mom smiled. She was clearly liking this idea of moving or else she was trying to use smile-power to convince us it wouldn't be so bad. That 'a little different' kept running through my head over and over, all day long. What exactly did that mean? Do they have running water and electricity in their houses? Is a house there just one big room we would all have to share? I remembered that my dad said it was modern, but *how* modern? Modern enough that we would be able to have a normal life?

Noah and I walked to school together like we always did, but this time it felt different. "Do they have sidewalks and do the kids go to schools like we do, Megan?" Noah wondered as he used his shoe to smush some weeds growing in the cracks in the sidewalk. I was wondering too.

"I guess so. Dad said it's not that different from here." I answered.

"How long will it take us to drive there?" Noah asked.

"Drive? I don't know. I think it's across the ocean. I think you might go on an airplane." I guessed. It seemed like anything that was *really* far away was going to be across an ocean. That made sense, right?

In school, I was fidgety. I could feel it and my teacher could too. At recess, she took me aside and asked what was up. I told her my parents had just told me that my family was moving to Israel and that I couldn't stop thinking about it.

"Israel? Wow." was her response. "That'll be a change!" I wasn't sure if her response meant she thought it was good or bad. Maybe she was as clueless as I was about Israel. "How comforting", I thought sarcastically, "exactly what I needed to hear"—as if the change wasn't what was worrying me in the first place. It didn't seem like she had anything else to say, so I asked if I could go play.

On the playground, Erin, who's been my best friend since I started second grade, came over and asked why our teacher wanted to talk to me. Erin has short, straight black hair—almost a boy-cut—and she has big, brown eyes and amazing freckles that she hates. I will never understand how you can hate freckles.

"You're not going to believe this," I started. Actually, I wasn't quite sure I believed it either or whether I was ready to talk about it yet. I could make something up or tell her something that wasn't important. I debated what to say. Finally, I said, "She saw that I was upset and she asked me why. I told her that yesterday I found out that we're moving."

"Moving?" Erin looked at me. Her eyes looked so sad, as if she might start to cry. "Far?" she asked.

"Very far. We're moving to Israel." I said, realizing how sad that made me feel.

"That's not fair! You can't move!" Erin shouted at me. "We're best friends. Best friends don't leave each other!" She sounded angry, like my mom did when I used her brand-new lipstick once.

"I don't know. My dad… he's going to work there… and Elise. There are trials for her in Israel that they don't have anywhere else in the world." I tried to explain both to her and to myself.

"Well, you're not moving!" Erin said very authoritatively, as if she had some part in whether it would happen or not.

As upset as I felt in that moment, I also felt sort of mad at Erin for not being happy that I was going to get to go to a new place. If she were moving to France, I'd totally be thinking about how lucky she was to get to see the Eiffel Tower. What was she supposed to think I was going to be lucky to get to see? Camels? Were there any cool landmarks in Israel?

Chapter 2 - Learning, Waiting & Wondering

Even though Noah's my little brother, we're good friends most of the time. The only thing I can't stand about him is when he starts following me around when I have friends over. They all think he's so cute, that they start playing with him. It used to seem like they ended up playing with him more than with me. I talked to my mom about it. She didn't really understand at first, but she finally agreed to a two-part plan. Part one was that I would play with my friends in my room, instead of in the living room and part two was that, if my mom noticed he was following me around, she'd offer to do a puzzle or play a game with him. Now that I don't feel like he's stealing my friends, I sometimes even invite him to join in whatever we're playing. Some games really are more fun with more people. Learning a new language was another adventure that I thought would be better with Noah. If only Elise could join us too, it would be perfect.

On the way to our lesson, I was trying to figure out how learning a new language works. If you don't know any of the words, you must have to learn it in bits, like the word, "cake"—and then how do you ever learn to say, "I would like some cake?" or "This cake is a-ma-zing!" Maybe I couldn't learn a new language. This whole thing was so confusing... and kind of scary. What if we got to Israel and I couldn't talk to anyone?

That afternoon, at our Hebrew lesson, I found out that I was right about the not-driving to Israel part. We were definitely going to fly there and it was going to be a looooooong flight. Shira, the teacher, said it was about eleven hours. Eleven hours on a plane? That's a whole, entire day, longer than a day at school—including two recesses and lunch... and even walking both ways. I bet the plane would have to stop and get gas. Are there gas stations in the sky? My mom was going to have to pack a lot of snacks for us! I started to make a mental list of the snacks I should ask her to get. Making this mental list was making me hungry.

Before Shira started teaching us anything, she showed us pictures of Israel. There were palm trees and buildings with big stones on them—not bricks, much bigger and not as flat. She said that that's the way most of the buildings in Jerusalem, where she's from, are. She claimed they call it Jerusalem stone, but I think she made that up just because she's from

Jerusalem. She told us that some people think they look like gold during sunset and that they call Jerusalem, 'Jerusalem of Gold'. Yeah, sure.

I had to find out about landmarks—anything cool I'd be able to tell my friends that I would get to see. Shira's eyes lit up and she started telling us about the Old City and the Western Wall—and then about the fact that Jerusalem is a holy city for Christians, Jews and Muslims—and that it's the land of the Bible. She told us about Bethlehem and the Sea of Galilee and other places—she said Israel is a small country and that she was sure we would get to see those places— that none was more than a few hours' drive from wherever in Israel we'd be living.

When Shira was ready to start teaching us Hebrew, it was hard for Noah and me to get serious. It was partly because we had come straight from school, but also because we were so curious about what Israel would be like that Shira had to keep getting us back on track. She said we'd learn about Israel *while* we were learning Hebrew... She managed to teach us a few words, despite our being so distracted. We learned the words 'anee', which means 'me' and 'ahta', which means 'you'. The only problem is that there are two words for 'you'- one if you're a girl and one if you're a boy. *Ahta* is for a boy and *aht* is for a girl. And there's no word for 'are'. Instead, you say "You pretty" or "You tall" (reminds me of Cookie Monster or something). I could tell it was going to be super-confusing. The first sentence I made was ridiculously stupid and Noah and I cracked up in the car on the way home. I told Noah, *ahta anee*, which means 'You are me'. I don't know why it made us laugh so hard, but I had tears dripping down my face. Even my mom thought it was funny—or at least pretended she did.

My dad came home and I told him my sentence. I didn't know that he had already started learning Hebrew using some app on his phone and he knew what it meant. He laughed and told me how proud he was that we were learning. He said the beginning is hard, but that later you start getting the hang of a new language—and that you don't need to know **all** the words in a sentence to understand the general meaning.

During spring break, Noah and I went for *a lot* of extra Hebrew lessons. We finished learning the alphabet. In Hebrew it's called *Aleph Bet*, because those are the names of the first two letters. And then we started learning how to read backwards. Backwards – from right to left. That's how they write Hebrew, no joke. How can you ever get used to that? One more thing that's completely nuts—they have a freaky weird vowel system where the vowels are under the letters most of the time, but sometimes they're in other places—and, according to Shira, once you're past 2nd grade, they don't use them at all. She laughed and said that my dad's name, Mark, was a great example, because in Hebrew you could also read it *marak*, which means soup. I thought that was hilarious.

At my ballet lesson, I practiced saying *lemala - lemata*—up and down—as I went up on my toes and back down. I wondered if I could take ballet in Israel too. My mom came into the studio with Elise to pick me up. Elise seemed to always like watching me dance, sometimes I wondered if she wished she could dance too. I heard her talking to the ballet teacher about our move. The ballet teacher said that there is lots of ballet in Israel—and a famous dance company called *Bat Sheva. Bat,* which you say *baht,* means girl or age and *sheva* means seven. I thought that means it's for seven-year-olds, so I asked my mom about that and she said it's the name of the company and that it's unlikely that there's a famous dance company of seven-year-olds. True.

In our Hebrew lessons, we started to learn songs and we watched a DVD of a show in Hebrew. I didn't understand much. I've been reading since I was 5. Noah only started reading last year, but it seemed like he was able to read Hebrew faster than I was. To prove I was the smarter one—which I totally am—I practiced extra-hard and used an app on my tablet to check how I was doing. It was also good for checking words I didn't know, since it translates too. There was something fun about learning Hebrew—and by June, Noah and I were using it as our own secret language when we didn't want people to understand. Or maybe we used it when we wanted to show off... and maybe what we said didn't always make sense.

My dad flew to Israel to check out places where we could live. His new job was going to be in Tel Aviv—which you say *Tell-a-Veev*. I think that's a funny name for a city and I hoped I wouldn't have to tell my friends that that was where we were moving to. The other thing my dad was checking out was the best places for Elise to get all the treatments she needed—and places where she could try new ones.

We picked my dad up at the airport, anxious to see the presents he'd brought us. He nearly always bought us something when he went away. I also was curious about where we were going to live. My dad was bursting with things to tell my mom – about kids who have CP, like Elise, who were able to say words and even to draw pictures. Elise looked at my dad while he was talking, as if she understood everything he was saying, but I had no idea if she understood anything at all. If Elise could learn to talk like the kids my dad had seen, she would be more like a regular sister. That would be cool! It did seem only fair to give Elise the best chance to do whatever she could, even if it meant moving away from all my friends, especially Erin. My parents had gotten Elise into one trial in Boston, but it was cancelled when none of the kids improved after the first few months. One of the trials in Israel was accepting new kids with Cerebral Palsy and was using stem cells. I don't know what stem cells are, but I guess I will find out.

Noah kept interrupting my dad and asking questions that I thought were dumb, like, "Do they have ice cream there?" My parents would never take us to live in a country without ice cream! Duh!

When we got home, my mom ordered pizza, which is my all-time favorite dinner. She remembered to ask them to put extra cheese on mine, exactly the way I like it. Dad showed us what he had brought for us from Israel, while mom sliced some cucumbers and tomatoes in the kitchen. He said that it didn't make sense to buy us presents from there when we'd be living there in less than 2 months, so he had brought us each a magazine in Hebrew. That barely seemed like a gift, especially since it would take forever for my Hebrew to be good enough to read it. I said thank you as nicely as I could and then tucked it under my arm and hoped I'd forget about it. Later, when I went to my room and looked at it, I was surprised that I could actually read a bit. I didn't understand anything, but it was something—and some of the faces were those of American singers or actors. I told my dad I had tried to read it and that it hadn't worked out so well. My dad said that when you're learning a new language, it's not enough to learn the words, you have to learn the expressions too – and that maybe that was why I didn't understand things, even though I had looked plenty of words up in the dictionary.

While we ate, dad put his laptop on the table and showed us a video of our new neighborhood and our new house. We weren't going to live in Tel Aviv, we were moving to Modi'in—*Mow-Dee-Een*. My dad said it's a half hour train ride from Tel Aviv and that it's a much more kid-friendly place—Tel Aviv is a busy city and Modi'in is a suburb. It's also close to both Jerusalem and Tel Aviv, the two main places where Elise would be going for treatments. I was expecting to see a desert, with a tree here and there, and probably a few camels. What my dad showed us was more like what Shira had shown us – streets and buildings and a playground. Actually, the playground was super cool and huge, like the kind my mom used to drive us half an hour to get to when she felt like being extra-nice. At least that's what she said. It might have been because she wanted to sit and read a book with no one bugging her. I asked my dad how far the playground was from our house. He chuckled and told me it was right across the street and that because Modi'in is considered a safe city, Noah and I would be able to go there by ourselves. It turned out that there were short pedestrian tunnels at both ends of the park, so that we would only have to cross one not-so-busy street to get both to the park and to the shopping center, where my dad said we could get ourselves ice cream. I was beginning to like the idea of moving. Independence sounded good. I found myself looking forward to moving, even if Erin wouldn't be able to come and visit.

My mom went into the kitchen to get dessert. It was mint-chocolate-chip ice cream. My almost-favorite, only mint and cookies can beat that. I sat down next to Elise and held both her hands. "Maybe you'll learn to talk!" I told her. She gave a half smile. "It's going to be fun. An adventure!" I was never sure what Elise understood, but I was pretty sure she heard what I said and it seemed like it made her feel happy. I opened the magazine my dad had brought me and pretended to read it to Elise, making things up as I went along. I did make sure to turn the pages backwards, like in Hebrew, but I didn't bother reading any of the words.

The last two months of school both flew by and seemed to be endless. I guess it was because I really wished we could stay in our house where everything was familiar and comfortable and because I was dreading moving so much that I wanted to get it over with. I **was** excited too, but it was mixed with a lot of fear and worry.

The school year finally ended and my mom spent hours packing things up to take with us. Most of what ended up in the 12 suitcases we took was either Elise's 'gear' or clothes. We had an awesome yard sale where I was allowed to sell whatever I wanted. I made $17.63. The three cents were from 3 blue cats-eye marbles I sold for a penny each. Whatever we didn't sell, give away or throw out got packed up and put in storage. Even our dishes.

My grandparents were not happy that we were moving. We'd started doing video calls with them to test it out and see what it was like. They were also going to come to visit us in Israel after we'd settled in. The truth is that, since we lived far away, we didn't see them that often anyway. We'd see my mom's parents about 3 times a year and my dad's even less often. I guess it was mostly the idea of us being so far away. At the airport, Grandpop told me quietly, so my parents wouldn't hear, that as sad as he was that we were moving away, he was also more than a little jealous that I'd get to learn all about another place in the world. What he said made me feel much better about the move. I told him that I'd be sure to show him around when they came to visit. Grandmama cried a lot, which made me cry too, even though I was super-excited about getting on an airplane for the first time. Mom and Dad cried too as we said goodbye and headed off to our new adventure.

Chapter 3 - We're here, we're really here!

The plane trip was extra, super-duper long. I mean, I watched two whole movies and one-and-a-half TV shows. One was boring, so I quit in the middle. I ate two meals and still had plenty of time to color in my new coloring book. I found out that the airplane doesn't need to fill up gas on the way. You fly 11 hours straight. No breaks. No intermission. At least there are bathrooms on the plane. While my parents rested, I sat next to Elise and whispered to her, telling her all the things I was wondering about. Would I make new friends before the school year started or would I be bored all summer? Would I like my new school? Would I manage with the Hebrew? How much would I miss Erin and our old neighborhood? Would some treatment they could do for her in Israel help her be able to do more things for herself. She always liked my being close to her, even if she did all the listening. I held her hand and imagined what it would be like if she could do the things most kids her age can.

I have to admit that sometimes I hate the fact that so much of our lives revolve around Elise, but I know it isn't her fault. Sometimes I wonder what it would be like if I were the one trapped in a body I couldn't control; unable to tell anyone what I want or how I feel. Usually, if I start thinking about it, it makes me scared and so I never manage to think about it for very long.

Noah found some kid on the plane to play with. They both had game consoles and were playing some dumb game. The loud hum of the plane made me sort of drowsy and I couldn't wait for the flight to be over. I'm seriously not sure they can invent anything more boring than flying. You're stuck in a seat, there's nowhere to go, and the noise and motion makes you feel sort of sick. I always thought flying would be so fun, but it was only fun for about the first ten minutes. After that, boooooooring. When whoever was talking on the loudspeaker finally announced that it was time to put on the seat belts and the local temperature – 31 degrees – I was happy, excited and terribly confused. My parents said Israel was hot. 31 was cold. I asked my mom about this and she explained that in Israel they use Celsius and not Fahrenheit and that 31 was indeed hot.

We got off the plane ridiculously tired. If I hadn't been so excited, I would have fallen asleep standing up. It didn't matter that I might have slept a little on the plane. I had never known it was possible to be that tired.

The first thing I noticed after we got off the plane and into the terminal was that there were plenty of signs in English. Cool. Maybe things wouldn't be as confusing as I thought they would be. We walked for about a mile until we got to passport control and then we went to wait six hundred hours for our suitcases. Waiting for suitcases isn't fun. After standing by the carousel for a few minutes, watching duffel bags and suitcases in every color of the rainbow go by, I told my parents we'd wait by the vending machines. I took Elise's stroller and Noah followed me. The drinks cost 10 Shekel, which my mom said was way-too-expensive, even though I was getting thirsty. I was almost afraid to sit down, in case I fell asleep before they got back to us. People kept shoving up in front of my parents and it seemed like even if our suitcases did come around that they would never be able to get them. Somehow, they finally did and we were on our way!

When we got out of the airport, a van was waiting to take us to our new house. That was lucky, because we had tons of suitcases and the van was a special one that let Elise stay in her stroller – meaning no one had to pick her up, fold up the stroller and everything – that was awesome, especially since it always takes so long and I was anxious to see our new house. I also understood as soon as we were outside of the airport that my mom was right. It **was** hot outside – and soooo muggy.

I got to sit by the window in the van. Everything looked normal. I mean, it was different, but there were bridges and highways and then we drove through a tunnel. There wasn't a camel in sight. It was not at all what I had expected. After a pretty short ride, maybe 15 minutes, my dad announced, "We're here!" We had arrived in Modi'in. There was a boulevard lined with palm trees on both sides and a ginormous Israeli flag. Except for the flag, it reminded me of movies of Florida, just not as flat.

A few minutes later we pulled up outside a building. Our new house! Except it wasn't a house – it was an apartment building. The van driver, who'd been chatting with my dad the whole way, helped us get our luggage into the apartment and my mom took Elise up in the elevator. The elevator was just big enough for the stroller and maybe two people. It was seriously tiny.

I was proud of myself because I came downstairs twice and took three suitcases up! It was only then that I got a real look at the apartment. How can I say this? It was small. I wasn't expecting it to be big, but this was a shock. The kitchen was like a little corner of our kitchen at home. The bathroom was barely big enough to fit a toilet, a sink and a bathtub. For a moment, I pictured myself accidentally taking a step back when I was brushing my teeth and falling into the bathtub. It was that small. The floors were beige tiles that looked like they had lots of little stones in them and the walls were all white. It was very different from our house—not in a good way.

The furniture was old and beat up, nothing we would ever have had in our house back home. Apparently, we were waiting for our new furniture to be delivered – this junk was temporary, my mom assured me. *Good*, I thought, *because it's hideously ugly*. I smiled to myself, feeling a little mean.

Before checking out the bedrooms, I looked out the big glass window in the living room and saw that across the street was the school my parents had told us about. My dad said that a little farther up were both the park he'd shown us and the shopping center. We kind of took a look around the apartment and talked about starting to unpack, but no one really felt like it and Noah seemed to be a little stir-crazy, so my dad suggested we take a walk.

I'm used to it being chilly in the evening, so I ran to get my sweater. My dad said that he didn't think I'd need it... We crossed the street, walking behind the school. It turned out that we were going to go to that school – right across the street from our house, meaning we could leave at like two-seconds-to-the-bell and still get there on time. After we walked past the school, there was a long path. There were stone walls on either side of the path and Noah jumped up and walked on the one on the right. At the end of the path you could either keep going straight, up a ramp, or left, toward a little tunnel. My dad said that if we went through the tunnel, we wouldn't have to cross the street.

Noah jumped down from the wall and grabbed my hand, pulling me toward the tunnel. It was a short tunnel, colored on both sides with spray paint – not exactly graffiti, but not exactly art either. Then something strange happened. I started to see orange sparkles all around us in the tunnel. Noah just kept going, so I followed him, but I wondered what the sparkles were. At the other side of the tunnel was the park my dad had shown us. There was a rink on the left, where kids were rollerblading and riding bikes; and swings on the right. Ahead of us was a huge structure with wood and ropes and slides. I was dizzy just looking at it.

Mom and dad sat on a bench with Elise beside them and Noah and I went to check out the playground. We found a little house with a bench inside and sat there. I told Noah that could be our hiding place in the park, since no one could see us. A few minutes later, Noah said he was thirsty, so we went back to the bench to find mom and dad.

My mom was talking to a woman – in English – and then she called me over and said, "Here's Megan!"

She turned to me and said, "Dena has a daughter your age who speaks English. Her name is Gali."

"Cool." I said, not knowing what to say.

My mom and Dena set up for Gali and me to meet at the park the next day. A reason to come back to the park was definitely a good thing!

Just when I realized I was starting to feel hungry, my dad said we could start our Israel experience right by eating *falafel* on our first night. *Falafel* is deep-fried ground chickpeas, with a few other things, that are rolled into balls. Shira had taught us about *falafel* and even showed us pictures. It turns out that both the balls are called *falafel* and when they put the balls into a pita with other things—like *hummus*, salad and *tehina*—it's still called *falafel*. I guess it's sort of like a burger—you'd call the burger a burger whether it's in a bun or not...

We walked through the park and then through another, kind of stinky tunnel, straight to the shopping center. There was a big supermarket and a bunch of smaller stores, including a *falafel* stand. My dad bought us each a *falafel* and a half-blue, half-purple slush. I never would have mixed two types of slush together, but all the kids were doing it, so I figured, why not? It was pretty good and I love the feeling of the cold slush going down my throat!

Now about *falafel*. It is messy. They take a pita, put some *hummus* in, then some falafel balls, then salad, then more falafel balls, then sauerkraut and fries and pickles and then they drizzle *tehina* on top. Not all of this actually fits into the pita and, while you're eating, as my mom says, the floor eats with you. It actually tasted great and I was surprised at how all those different foods mixed together actually works. I must have been hungry, because, except for my dad, I was the first one to finish it.

When we finished eating, we walked back home and got ready for bed. I was so excited that I knew I'd never be able to fall asleep, but the next thing I knew, the sun was up and my mom was telling me that it was time for breakfast.

Chapter 4 - Independence

My mom had gone out and gotten fresh croissants and chocolate milk for breakfast. I sat down on one of the mismatched Formica chairs, each a different fakey wood-grain, and took a paper plate and a croissant. Surprisingly, it was still warm. Even more surprisingly, it was filled with melted chocolate, which didn't seem like the healthy kind of breakfast my mom liked to give us – but I definitely wasn't going to bring that up. I didn't feel like drinking chocolate milk – all that sweetness was too much for me in the morning – so I got a cup of water. You should just know – tap water in Israel isn't always cold. It was room temperature and tasted gross. I drank it anyway, but I decided to remember that before drinking water from the faucet again.

I took a look around the house. Lots of unpacked suitcases, hardly any visible floor, and Elise sitting in her stroller. Noah was finished eating and half-sitting, half lying down on the beat-up couch playing with his game console.

"What time is it?" I asked my mom. If you've ever heard of jet lag, it's real. It makes you feel confused and completely lose your sense of time.

"Around 8:30." My mom answered, as she took some measuring spoons out of the housewares suitcase and put them in the kitchen drawer. I was used to my dad being out, but then my mom spent most of her time with Elise – so now, if my dad wasn't home and my mom was unpacking, it seemed to me that the only right thing to do was to ask my mom if she needed some help... I had nothing better to do anyway.

I could tell my mom was surprised that I asked if I could help, which made me feel proud of myself. She said I should take Noah and go pick up some sponges and cleaning spray, since she wanted to give the kitchen a more thorough cleaning – and maybe a new broom and dustpan. She handed us money and told us to get ourselves slush or a popsicle on the way home. There was just one problem. The money in Israel is different. They use Shekels and not Dollars and a Shekel is only worth about 25 cents. I could see how being good at math was going to come in handy. The coins are also different. My mom had given me a 50 Shekel bill and a 10 Shekel coin, which is worth about $2.50. The 50 was for the groceries and the 10 was for us to buy whatever we wanted!

Noah looked at me and we gave each other a thumbs-up. This was going to be fun. Being able to go buy something alone was cool.

We went down the elevator and crossed the street. It looked like a big, wide street. Two lanes. There was practically no traffic, so we waited until there were no cars in sight and then we crossed. We walked down the path and then when we got to the place where we could go either up the ramp or through the tunnel, I remembered that I was still curious about those sparkly orange lights I'd seen the day before in the tunnel. I had probably imagined them because I was so tired... No one else seemed to have seen them.

Noah was just plain happy. He was smiling and unusually quiet. Maybe he was feeling that same sense of freedom I was. It was kind of like being a butterfly fresh out of the cocoon, free to explore everything for the first time in a completely different way. We got to the tunnel and we were holding hands, swinging them back and forth together. The orange sparkles started again and then they got so strong that I had to close my eyes.

I opened my eyes about two seconds later – and we weren't in the tunnel anymore. It looked like we were in some sort of cave with glittery orange walls. Unlike outside, where it had been pretty warm, it was comfortably cool. Noah and I both turned around, our eyes open wide, completely confused by what we were seeing.

"Is this real?" Noah finally managed to ask.

"I think so..." I hesitated. Could we really just close our eyes for a second and be somewhere completely different? That made no sense...

"But where are we – and how do we get back to where we were?" Noah had put my thoughts into words.

"I have no idea…" I said, feeling scared and confused. My stomach started to hurt.

A piece of paper flew down from above, swishing left and right and finally landing at our feet. Noah picked it up. I could see something was written on it and my first thought was that if it was a message in Hebrew, we were in deep trouble, because my Hebrew wasn't that good.

It wasn't. It was a message that seemed to be handwritten, in English:

Here you can do more

"Here you can do more? More what?" I asked. "What does that even mean?" I was annoyed; cryptic things frustrate me. Noah was intrigued. I was trying to understand how we were going to get out of there.

"Maybe jump higher?" He tried to jump. He was right; he had definitely just jumped higher than anyone I'd ever seen jump – except maybe in a sports competition.

"Wow!" I said, shocked.

"Yeah, wow! I wonder what else!" Noah said.

I'd always wanted to sing, but my voice was never that smooth or strong... I started to belt out my favorite song. It sounded good. I mean REALLY good. My stomach hurt a little less, but I was still anxious about being stuck wherever it was we were—and I was completely unsure where that was... On top of that, I remembered that we were on our way to get some stuff for my mom and that she was going to start worrying about us – especially since we were new here and we might not know our way around – she might think we were lost... This was the worst day of my life. What were we going to do? I looked at Noah's watch. 8:35.

"Did you set your watch since we got to Israel?" I asked him.

"Yup. Dad set it for me this morning before he left."

I was baffled. It couldn't be that just 5 minutes had passed since I finished breakfast.

"Let's try something else, Megan!" Noah urged.

"Like what?" I seemed to be out of ideas.

"Like, let's talk to each other in Hebrew." Noah suggested.

"Um... OK..." and he started talking. Part of my brain knew that he was saying words I'd never heard before, but another part of my brain knew that I could understand what he was saying. Then, I heard my own voice speaking words that I only understood as they came out. It was the strangest experience I had ever had.

"Noah, I said, this is fun and all, but I'm really scared about how we get out of this place and go home." I was starting to feel a cold sweat creep up on me and my stomach was doing flips.

In front of us, a hallway we hadn't seen before appeared, brightly lit, with blue sparkles. We started to walk down it. It seemed to go on for quite a while and I started to get scared. I turned around to look back to where we had been before, but I couldn't see the orange sparkles anymore. I grabbed Noah's hand tightly and said – even though I didn't believe it at all—"We're OK." I was being the responsible big sister. "Let's think together. There's got to be some way to get out of here..." Noah gave me a silly face, trying to cheer me up. How was he not worried?

Another piece of paper swished out of nowhere and fell in front of us. This time, it was in Hebrew, and by some miracle, I could read and understand it. *Together, you're stronger* it said.

וחי זי חלקים אחד רוני

"Stronger? That means if we want to get out, we need to work together, right? But what does it have to do with strength?"

 An area in the wall appeared to be very subtly blinking.

"Maybe we need to push on the wall or something?" Noah and I went to the blinking spot and pushed on the wall at the same time. Clearly this was a stupid idea, but I didn't have a better one. To my complete surprise, the blue sparkles became orange and then got almost blindingly bright. We both closed our eyes.

When Noah and I opened them, I was afraid what we'd see, but we were back in the tunnel. The notes I had been holding had disappeared.

Chapter 5 - What was that?

There was no question that I had just had the strangest experience of my life. Jet lag could certainly do strange things to a person. It was the jet lag, right? I'd ask Noah, he'd give me one of his "Are you nuts?" faces, have no idea what I was talking about and within a few days, once I got over my jet lag, everything would be normal. We'd pick up the things my mom wanted, go home and then I'd unpack my suitcase. I just had to get it through my head that being really tired could make my mind play crazy tricks on me. Everything was fine—or was it?

"What was THAT?" Noah half-exclaimed, half-asked.

I considered pretending not to know what he was talking about, but found myself answering honestly, "I have absolutely no idea."

"Megan? Was it magic? Do you believe in magic?" Noah asked me in the most innocent way.

"I, um, I don't… but I… I can't explain…" I stammered. I was trying to collect my thoughts. What Noah said made sense – that it was magic – only I didn't actually believe in magic.

"I think it was magic." Noah said. "The tunnel is absolutely magical." He said it like it was an easy thing to accept.

We walked a bit and sat back down on one of the benches near where my mom and dad had waited for us the day before. I felt out of breath and it was hot outside. I peeked at Noah's watch again. It was 8:37.

"What are we going to do?" I asked Noah. "I mean, everyone knows there's no such thing as magic. Maybe we need to tell mom and she'll take us to a doctor or something."

Noah gave me his, "Are you serious?" face. "We didn't just both suddenly get sick and start having weird visions together." Before I could interrupt, Noah continued, "And it isn't the jet lag either. It really happened."

"Try jumping now." I said, anxious to make sure everything was back to normal.

Noah jumped. He jumped higher than he should have been able to. He didn't jump as high as he had in the sparkly place, but it was still freaky. He noticed too.

"So, can we still speak better Hebrew than before?" Noah wondered.

"Maybe." How was I supposed to know? Trying to wrap your head around something like this when it's hot outside and you have jet lag is harder than smiling while you're eating okra. Impossible, probably. "We'll figure it out later." I told Noah. "Let's go get the stuff mom wanted."

We continued walking through the park and went to the supermarket to buy the things my mom asked for. Then we stopped at the candy store, where the guy mixed 3 different kinds of slush in the same cup for each of us. He told us that next time we could do it ourselves if we wanted.

Noah and I started walking through the stinky tunnel into the park, when I suddenly realized that I'd talked to the guy at the candy store in Hebrew. I used the word *barad*, which means 'hail' to ask for the slush... and he understood me. It made no sense.

"Noah," I asked. "Did you notice that I spoke to the guy in Hebrew?"

Noah took another sip of his slush and said, "Nope."

Weird. I thought to myself. Maybe some of the Hebrew had stuck too. Could magic help you learn a language?

My mom was proud of us when we got home. Proud that we'd gotten exactly what she needed and, I guess, proud that we were able to do it on our own. I walked over to Elise and put the straw of my slush in her mouth so she could sip some. I could tell she liked it, so I sat next to her and gave her a few more sips.

"How's the weather outside?" my mom asked.

"It is so hot, I thought I might melt." I told her. It never got that hot where we used to live, at least not so early in the morning. I was thankful for the ceiling fan above my head. Even though the air conditioning was on, I needed the extra breeze.

"Did you have any trouble?" I heard my mom ask, as a jumble of thoughts started to fill my head. Trouble?

Hmm. I mean – was being suddenly in a different place from where I was a second before after being practically blinded by lights no one but Noah and I seemed to see considered trouble?

"Nope." Noah said simply. OK. I guess that meant I didn't have to answer. Having a little brother could be convenient...

I tried to put the whole tunnel thing out of my head and I took Elise to the new tiny room we shared. The room was rectangular and because of its size and where the door and closet were, there were very few ways to arrange it. My bed was on one wall, Elise's on the other. Between the beds, there was space that wouldn't even be wide enough for another bed – maybe 3 feet—and on one wall, there was a freestanding closet, with shelves and hanging space. It could probably hold about half of what my closet back in US could hold – and I had to share it with Elise. The room was so small that there was no way I could fit in even a small desk. I guessed that meant homework at the kitchen table.

I tried to keep myself from being upset about how tiny the room was and started unpacking my clothes as I told Elise a story about princesses who turn into frogs and end up deciding that being a frog is much more fun. It ended with them hopping around a fountain happily, avoiding princes whenever they came by. When I finished unpacking my clothes, I took another suitcase and unpacked some of Elise's. I wanted to take a break and do something else, but I couldn't think of anything to do and it was definitely too hot to be outside.

"Can I call Erin now?" I asked my mom.

"You could, but I don't think she'd appreciate it very much." My mom said half-laughing.

"Why?" I didn't get it.

"It's 4:30 in the morning there." Mom was finished organizing the kitchen and was unpacking her clothes. "Seven-hour time difference."

"Seriously? No wonder I'm so tired!" I said. But it wasn't a regular kind of tired I was feeling. It was almost like being sick. Wanting to be awake and asleep and to throw up all at the same time.

"Maybe we can go to the mall." My mom said.

"Mall? They have malls here?" I was genuinely surprised.

"It's at the other end of this street. Not very far, but too far to walk with Elise in this heat." My mom told me as she picked up her cellphone and started dialing. "I'll get us a taxi."

The taxi was waiting outside within five minutes and it was about a three-minute drive to the mall. The driver helped with Elise as if he did it ten times a day and he smiled at us and said "Welcome to Israel!"

In the mall, we had to go through a security-screening like at the airport. My mom handed the security guard her purse and her keys and then walked through one of those metal detector things. Elise was allowed to go around it and Noah and I walked right through. I asked my mom about it and she said that that's just the way things are in Israel – and that we would get used to it.

The elevator in the mall was glass and I love glass elevators. It was cool to see all the stores even before the doors opened. The mall was smaller than the one back home, but it was pretty. There was a display that looked like huge, colored origami balls hanging from the top of the second floor of the mall and most of the store names were written in English.

We ate lunch at the mall and then took another taxi home. I was more than ready for a nap. It seemed we all were. As soon as we got home, we all hopped into our beds and fell asleep.

The next sound I heard was my mom waking me up. "Megan, Megan," she half-whispered, "wake up! Remember you're meeting Gali today."

"Mmmmrrmrr..." I growled. I was only partly awake. "Oh. Park. Right." I felt myself waking up, getting out of my bed and going to wash my face. I was still only half-awake, but my body knew what to do.

"What time is it?" I asked my mom.

"Almost 4." She told me. Four. In the afternoon. It had to be. My body was so confused. I never slept in the afternoon.

"OK. I'm ready." I said, slipping my feet into my sandals. "Where's Noah?"

"In the kitchen, why? You want him to come with you?" My mom sounded surprised. Maybe it was because she was so used to my complaining that he always tagged along.

"Yes, sure, why not?" I said. It seemed like it would be easier to meet someone new with Noah than alone.

Noah was more than happy to come along. It was still boiling hot outside and my mom made us take water bottles with us. We were going to look like the biggest dorks on the planet, but we had no choice. There was no point arguing with my mom about something like this. At least she didn't make us put on sunscreen—she said you don't need sunscreen after 4. I figured that must be some weird Israeli rule.

We avoided the tunnel on the way to the park. It was all too confusing and risking the magic again just seemed too... well, risky, I guess. On the benches where we'd sat earlier, we saw Dena and her daughter, Gali.

Gali was carrying a water bottle too, which made me feel less dorky. Maybe that's just what kids do in Israel. We talked and played for a while. It was almost the same as being back home. Gali spoke English and she was interested in hearing about the United States. She'd never been there. I told her about my bedroom and she said it sounded like one of those rooms in movies. I told her about my school and about baseball games—she only kind of knew what baseball was—and about my friend Erin, who had a pet ferret. Her mom looked ferret up on her phone to show her a picture. It's called a *khamos,* but even after knowing that, she had no idea what it was. I guess there aren't too many ferrets in Israel. I pretended to be holding it and showed her how it ran up my arm and around the back of my neck and we both laughed.

I took Gali's phone number, since my mom said I was going to get my own cellphone and told her I'd message her as soon as I got my phone.

On the way home, Noah wanted to through the tunnel again. I would say that the thought of going there scared me, but it would only be half-true. I was both terrified and curious. I decided Noah was right. We had to try it again to see if it would happen again—and, if it did, what else we could find out about it.

Chapter 6 - A Magic Tunnel?

Noah and I must have had what my mom calls 'an adrenaline rush', because even though I had felt so tired that I was dizzy, as soon as we had decided we were going to the tunnel, we both took off running. We got to the tunnel, looked at its sides and didn't see anything strange. There was some weird graffiti on the wall, but nothing other than that – and I had seen that the first time we were there.

"Maybe we need to go in from the other direction? That's what we did last time..." I thought aloud.

"OK, let's try it." Noah said.

We walked through the tunnel, turned around and went back in. Still nothing. I was partly relieved, since it meant that maybe it was just some weird experience, but partly disappointed, since I felt like it would be pretty cool if we could do more of that "doing more". I had sort of hoped we'd get to experience some more magic.

"We need to try again," Noah said, "but this time, swinging our hands together like last time."

"OK." I grumbled. "I'm sure that has nothing to do with it, but whatever."

We walked into the tunnel swinging our hands together and there they were—the orange sparkles that got brighter and brighter until we had to close our eyes. In a moment, we were in the orange sparkly room again!

I gave Noah an embarrassed "You were right" look, but he wasn't gloating, he was just in awe. "Oh my gosh!" Noah yelled. "This is soooo cool!" He started jumping way up high over and over. Then he did a flip in the air. "I can do ANYTHING!" he shouted happily.

I wondered what I should try to do. I suddenly noticed a few hallways leading out of the orange room. They were all sparkling and each one was a different color. So much temptation...

"Want to try the pink hallway?" I asked Noah.

"Pink is for girls!" He said, doing another flip in the air.

I made a face. "Green?" I suggested.

"OK. Green." Noah agreed. He didn't sound too excited about it – those flips must have been awfully fun for him.

The green hallway widened as we walked in. The sparkles all over the side reminded me of a Christmas tree covered in dew. I noticed a smell kind of like freshly cut grass. I was caught up in thought when I saw that Noah was jumping.

He jumped and it was clearly not as high as it had been before, in the orange room. "So... the different color must mean something different." I thought. A piece of paper swirled down in front of me. I bent down to pick it up, realizing that I didn't care what language it was in.

Here you can understand more

"Here, you can understand more? Understand more what?" Noah wondered aloud.

"I have no idea." I said, feeling all my dizzy, tired confusion crashing down on me at once. "What do we not understand?"

"I don't know…" Noah said. "Maybe we should just go back to the orange room and do some flips."

I was going to go along with what Noah wanted regardless of how tired I suddenly felt, but when we turned around to head back to the orange room, it wasn't there anymore. There didn't appear to be any way out of the green room. Panic started to set in as I realized we were stuck. Again.

I tried to calm myself down. "We've gotten out before; we'll get out again." I promised myself silently. It was only slightly convincing. I repeated it over and over in my head.

To Noah, I half-asked, half-said, "Can we just go home?" I didn't want him to know how panicky I felt.

"We can't go home before we do something magical!" Noah insisted.

"I'm so tired. All I want to understand right now is my bed..." I said.

"I.... I want to understand why Hebrew is written backwards!" Noah laughed as if he didn't expect any sort of explanation. "It's so dumb!"

"To confuse people like us!" I said. "Can we go?"

"C'mon, Megan... Stop worrying so much!" Noah pleaded. "Let's at least wait for an answer." A few seconds later he sounded surprised, "Ohmigosh! I know it!"

"Huh?" I asked.

"I mean no one knows for sure, but they think it might have to do with ancient writing using tools that were easier to use from right to left." Noah explained. He was as shocked as I was.

"That's wild!" I said. "I wish I could think what I even want to understand. Can we go now?" I was falling asleep standing up. I thought if I closed my eyes even for a few seconds I'd be sleeping heap on the floor.

"OK. But promise you'll come back with me again really soon." Noah demanded in his cutest voice.

"I promise." What choice did I have? Of course, I wanted to come back too.

"You think we just have to push on the wall again?" Noah asked.

"Let's try." I said, as we put our hands against the wall and started to push. For some reason, I suddenly understood it would work.

In a moment, after being nearly blinded by orange sparkles, we were back in the tunnel.

"So it IS magic." I admitted to myself and to Noah. "Magic is real! And it's SO cool!"

Chapter 7 - Understanding More

Our mom was at the door, holding a cake and talking to a woman I didn't know when we got home.

"This is Noah," my mom said, running her fingers through his hair, "and this is Megan, my oldest," she said, putting her hand on my shoulder.

"Hi!" Noah and I said together and then looked at each other and cracked up. We'd even used exactly the same tone.

The little kid clinging to the back of her jeans was *Ofriki.* I'm not kidding. These people called their kid something that sounds like, "oh, freaky!" I hope for his sake that his family never relocates – at least not to a country where people speak English! Later, I found out that his real name is Ofri, but apparently everyone calls him Ofriki. The mom, Ronit, *row, neat* had brought over a cake to welcome us to the building. They lived downstairs and said we should let them know if we need anything. I was tempted to say we need to add a staircase and take over their apartment, because ours is too small, but I wasn't sure she would think that was funny. Ronit asked us how we like Israel so far and Noah answered that he thought it's a very cool place. Cool sounded like the wrong word, considering we were standing by the door, where the air conditioning didn't quite reach us. Ronit wanted to know if I babysat, so my mom explained that I'm only 11, so I definitely don't babysit yet. I asked if there were any other girls my age in the building. Ronit said she wasn't sure, that maybe on the third floor there was a family with a kid my age, but she couldn't remember whether the kid was a boy or a girl.

After Ronit left, we tasted the cake she made. It was better than I expected. Very chocolatey.

"Nice neighbor," my mom said.

"Yup. If you live in a building do all the neighbors bring you cake?" I wondered.

"I guess we'll find out!" my mom said, collecting the plates and taking them to the sink.

That night, our second night in Israel, I lay in my bed thinking. I was trying to figure out what I was supposed to understand more about. I thought about school subjects. Math – no, definitely not that, since I thought math was the easiest subject in school. History – maybe, since I didn't understand why it was important to know details of things that happened hundreds of years ago. As I continued to go through the subjects one-by-one, I found myself less and less able to focus... My thoughts drifted everywhere.

I woke up to hear Elise breathing softly across the room and I suddenly knew. I wanted to understand more about Elise. About what she understood, what she felt, what she wanted, what she liked. Maybe the magic tunnel could help me get to know my little sister better—I'd always wanted to, but I could never figure out how.

I came to a realization. We were going to have to take Elise to the magic tunnel.

I started making plans in my head, thinking of how we would get Elise there and what we would need to do to figure out what we were supposed to understand. I couldn't wait for morning to come.

It was Noah who woke me up. He was standing by my bed wearing his favorite red t-shirt that said on it, "I'm 7. Beware! 7 8 9!" I thought the shirt was totally stupid, but he'd gotten it from his friend Lena, who he was totally in love with, for his birthday, so he thought it was the coolest thing ever. Have I mentioned that Noah is 8?

"Ready? Let's go!" He said.

"Ready? Do I look ready?" I asked annoyed. "No. I'm not ready." My mom calls it my 'morning grumpy tone'.

"Well, GET ready!" Noah sounded hyper.

"Wait." I said, rubbing my eyes and stretching. "I had an idea."

"Shoot!" Noah said, sounding a little too much like my mother.

"We have to take Elise with us." I said.

"Elise?" Noah sounded surprised. "What can SHE do there?" and then, about two seconds later, his jaw dropped. "Do you think...?" He left the question open.

"Mm hmm." I nodded. "I do."

"Ohmigosh – this could be amazing!" Noah sounded far more excited than I'd thought he would be. He rarely spent time with Elise, so I was surprised that he thought it was such a good idea.

I got ready quickly and then we both shoved a few spoons of cereal down our throats as fast as we could.

"Mom," I said, trying not to sound suspicious, "We're going to take Elise to the park. OK?"

My mom came into the room with a perplexed look on her face. "You want to take Elise?" She asked.

OK, so it wasn't like we offered to take Elise places very much. Actually, I couldn't think of a single case in which I'd offered to take her anywhere, except to the other room to read her a story. So, I guess despite my 'poker voice' I wasn't convincing.

"Yeah, well, Mom... You have lots of stuff to do and um... well, the park... it's... there are no stairs, so I think maybe Elise will enjoy seeing the park." I said. Yuck. I did a rotten job. My mom would never agree now.

"OK. Sure." My mom had bought it—or maybe she was just so happy to have a bit of a break. "But be home by 10. I'm taking Elise for an appointment in Jerusalem."

We put on baseball caps, prepared bottles of water and were ready at the elevator in about 3 minutes. All three of us.

"Have fun!" My mom smiled at us. I could see the proud look at the corners of her eyes and wondered momentarily if I should feel guilty for having tricked her. I decided not to. After all, I did have good intentions.

"Elise," I started quietly, the moment my mom closed the apartment door. "We're going to do something really, really cool. Something so amazing you won't even believe it."

Chapter 8 - Understanding Elise

We were so excited to see what Elise would be able to do or what we would be able to understand that we got to the tunnel as fast as we possibly could. When we got there, Noah and I each took one of Elise's hands and pulled her along with her stroller. I practically held my breath, hoping that it would work. I closed my eyes as we walked into the tunnel, afraid the magic might be gone or that it would only work for two people at a time – maybe even only for

Noah and me. I slowly opened my eyes. Sparkles. Orange sparkles and then bright lights. I looked at Elise and saw her squinting. Then the light became so bright I had to close my eyes. It worked again! This time, all three of us were in the orange sparkly room!

My mind was racing. What were those plans I'd made in the night? What should be the first thing to try? Noah was already busy doing flips in the air, which I found terribly distracting. "NOAH - stop! I need to focus!" I shouted at him. Then, I started quietly, "Elise, this room is special, it's magic." I talked to her the way I usually did, but then I realized that it felt different. I didn't usually expect her to understand me – and this time, I did. "You can do more things here than you usually can. Do you want to try to do something?"

Elise smiled at me. I took it as a yes. "OK, how about doing this?" I picked up my hand and waved bye-bye, like babies do, by opening and closing my fist. "Can you try?"

Elise smiled again. I raised my hand again, showing her, like I had probably hundreds of times over the past 4-1/2 years, how to wave bye-bye. I looked at Elise, so hopeful that she could do something, *anything* to show me that she could 'do more' like that first message we'd gotten. It had worked for Noah and for me, it should work for her too, right? I tried a third time and a fourth time – and then I saw her fingers move – just a little bit, but they moved forward and back. I was completely sure of it but I had to see it again.

"Great, Elise! Great! Now again!!!" I was super-excited.

I waved and her fingers moved. I kept doing it over and over. It was working, but I could also tell that her fingers weren't moving any more than the first time. Maybe it was time to try something else.

I showed her how to kick with her foot by pretending to kick an imaginary ball. Nothing. I tried waving bye-bye again – and her fingers moved just like before. Amazing, but we didn't seem to be making any progress. It was so hard to be patient.

"Noah?" I rolled my eyes at the new gymnastics freak. "We have to try the green room!"

He didn't look happy about it, but he walked with Elise and me toward the green glittery walls.

"Elise?" Noah surprised me by talking first, "What do you want to be able to do?"

Elise didn't speak, but her answer came into my head. "Dance."

Noah looked at her, "Really? You want to be able to dance?"

Ohmigosh, ohmigosh, he got it too! We had suddenly found a way into Elise's mind. Incredible. It wasn't a

voice, but maybe you could call it a 'communication'
– "I also want to be able to laugh."

Understanding these things was both devastating
and thrilling. I felt an almost physical pain knowing
that Elise wanted to do things that she couldn't, but I
was also incredibly excited and happy to know that
there was so much more inside Elise that we hadn't
gotten to know about yet – and I was really looking
forward to getting that chance.

"What's your favorite food?" I asked Elise.

"Melon."

"What song do you like?" Noah wondered.

"The Wheels on the Bus."

We asked a bunch more questions and it was like we
were interviewing someone who we both knew and
didn't know. Every answer seemed to make Elise
more and more like the sister I'd always wanted her

to be. The sister I had dreamed about when my mom and dad had first told me that we were going to have a new baby.

I started to worry that we were tiring Elise out. She never did very much and we were asking a lot of her. I wondered if she always communicated and we just couldn't hear it outside of the magic tunnel or if she was only communicating now. I couldn't imagine what it would be like not to be able to tell anyone what you think or feel. Did she understand us speaking only because we were here – or did she always understand us? Was Elise excited that we could understand her now? I had to know.

"Elise?" I asked. "When we talk at home. Do you understand us?"

It turned out that she mostly understood us and that she was excited that we could understand her now. She also communicated to us that she wanted to come back to the sparkly rooms. It was magical for her too. I wondered whether we should stay longer, try to find out more—or if we were sort of pushing our luck... Then, just like the previous times we were in the tunnel, I felt a sort of fear creeping up on me. My mom would say I was "antsy". I had the feeling we had to get out. A type of claustrophobia, I guess... or maybe the tunnel telling us it was time to go. I started getting worried—how were we going to push on the wall with Elise?

"Noah, I think we need to go..." I said. "I don't feel so good." I thought that if I looked in the mirror my face might be a little green.

Noah looked at me and said, "Well, we're going to come back later today then, OK?"

"OK," I replied.

I was relieved that Noah had agreed to leave without arguing with me. I really needed to get out of there.

"How will we do it?" I wondered aloud.

Noah, who I always expected to look for me to answers, took one of Elise's hands and I took the other and we pushed. Orange sparkles, bright lights and magically we were back in the tunnel.

Although it was incredibly hot outside, the open space made me feel good. I took a few deep breaths, as if I had been lacking oxygen. Checking Noah's watch, I saw that we had only been out with Elise for about 15 minutes. We would need to take her for longer than that for my mom to get anything done.

We walked into the park and sat down on the bench with the most shade we could find. Elise was facing us and smiling. I waved bye-bye at her, just like in the orange room, and stared at her fingers. At first, it was barely noticeable, but then, they moved ever so slightly. My heart skipped a beat.

Chapter 9 - Jerusalem

After taking a long walk around the park and getting ourselves rainbow slushes, we went home.

My mom was happy to see us and she was a little stressed about getting out of the house in time for Elise's first appointment in Jerusalem. I hadn't thought about it and my mom hadn't mentioned it, but it turned out that Noah and I were going along. That must have also been a jet lag thing—otherwise

I would have been super-excited about going to Jerusalem!

We still didn't have a car and my mom said she was a little afraid to drive anyway, so we went by taxi. The taxi driver asked my mom if she wanted to go on 443 or 1 and I had no idea what he was talking about. I guess my mom did. She said she wanted to go on the Tel Aviv Jerusalem road because she'd heard it was safer. Weren't taxi drivers supposed to decide how to get somewhere? After that, the driver was busy loudly talking on his phone most of the time, so he didn't say much to us. Exactly the opposite of the taxi driver who had taken us the day before.

We drove past the mall—a place I recognized(!)—and then were out of the city within a few minutes. I saw a huge park with a pond on the right. There was a climbing area with giant wooden structures. I thought I even spotted a fountain and some pedal boats.

The scenery got very green and we drove past a place called Park Canada and then past a monastery—the Latrun Monastery. Latrun reminded me of 'latrine' – and I thought that was pretty funny. My mom explained that Jerusalem is at a higher altitude than Modi'in, so that we'd be going uphill a lot of the way. I didn't really notice. I couldn't wait to see that gold dome that I'd seen in the pictures.

We got to the hospital without ever seeming to get to a city. It was more like driving on highways and then past a little town and then straight to the hospital. The taxi driver dropped us off and we had to go through security to get into the hospital—except Elise. There was a special entrance for her in her stroller. All this security was weird. We headed toward the information desk and then to the Neurology clinic. We waited for a long time and Noah and I didn't know what to do. We were bored and started goofing off and my mom got mad at us and told us to sit still. I tried, but it didn't work so well.

Every time I looked at Noah, he made another silly face at me and I couldn't help laughing. My dad refers to it as 'giggle-mode'.

After about an hour, the doctor finally called my mom and Elise in. We stayed outside, with instructions from my mom to be quiet. A woman, maybe a nurse, told us that there's a playroom down the hall and that she'd tell our mom that we were there. I wondered why she remembered this only now. Maybe our noise wasn't bothering her as much as my mom thought it was. I was happy to have something to do, so Noah and I went and played there. In the play area, we saw a little boy who was two or three years old and had darkish skin. He was speaking a language that I didn't recognize as Hebrew. His mom was with him, wearing a black scarf that covered her head and neck. I pinched Noah gently to get his attention and asked him what language the boy was speaking. Noah, not known for his shyness, walked up to the boy's mom and asked her if she spoke English. She didn't. Hebrew?

"*Ktzat.*" She said – 'a little bit'.

"*Safa?*" Noah asked – meaning 'language'.

"*Aravit.*" She answered – 'Arabic'.

"*Magniv.*" Noah responded with the slang word for 'cool'.

After that, Noah and I kept on playing. The toys there were for kids much smaller than we were, but it was nice not to have anyone shushing us.

When I thought about it later, I realized that with just 4 words, Noah and the Arab woman were able to have some sort of conversation. This made me think how *magniv* it could be if Elise could learn to say even a few words.

After the appointment, my mom got us ice cream from a vending machine. I got an ice cream sandwich and Noah got a cone, which turned out to be a better choice, because the entire cone was lined with chocolate on the inside. Elise ate a popsicle. My mom who always prefers a bite of someone else's food to buying something for herself, took a bite from Noah's and then from mine and then, wiping her lips with a tissue, said we might as well see some of Jerusalem. My friends were going to be so jealous!

We got into another taxi and my mom asked the driver to drive us around the old city. I didn't understand why she wanted to go to the old city, since it seemed like the kind of place that would be ugly and run down. It wasn't.

What we saw were these amazing walls, like those of a castle. I understood now that what Shira had told us about Jerusalem stone was true. It does sort of remind you of gold. We drove past some amazing, high stone gates and then uphill to a place called Mount Scopus. There, my mom told Noah and me to get out of the car and look straight ahead. In front of me, I saw the gold dome on, what my mom told me, is called the Temple Mount. The dome itself is called The Dome of the Rock. I know, it sounds weird. It was an amazing view. I mean, really incredible. I finally understood what people mean when they say that something "takes your breath away". Wow. After about five minutes of my eyes being glued to the view, I got back into the car to sit with Elise and my mom got out and stood beside Noah to look.

Elise smiled at me and I asked her quietly, "Do you remember?" and then I waved bye-bye at her and looked at her hands. Her fingers moved just the slightest bit, but something about the fact that she could still do it gave me hope that the *do more* magic would work on Elise too. Maybe each time it would make a little more difference.

When my mom & Noah got back into the taxi, we started to drive back to Modi'in. I was disappointed that our time in Jerusalem was over, but my mom promised we would come back many times.

We drove on a different road and passed by some Arab villages and a lot of rocky hills. I mean, the hills were covered with huge rocks, instead of trees or bushes or anything green. Unlike the other road we'd been on, this one reminded me of a desert – as if it didn't rain on this part of the country. After about half an hour, we got to a place that looked sort of like toll booths. Apparently, they have checkpoints on this road and if you look suspicious, they make sure it's OK for you to go through. I guess we didn't look suspicious, because they let us go right past them. Pretty soon after that, we turned left into Modi'in.

I remembered the palm tree-lined road and knew we were close to our new home. Everything was so different that it was like being on vacation. Maybe that made it easier to be away from everything that was familiar.

When we got home, we were all thirsty, so we sat in the living room and had some ice water. I asked my mom what the doctor had said about Elise and she told me that the team was going to discuss Elise's case and come up with a treatment plan – that she didn't mind explaining it to me, but that it would be easier if I could just wait until my dad got home so she wouldn't have to explain everything twice.

I started thinking about the magic tunnel again and, for some reason, that reminded me of Grandpop. I got out my tablet and checked what time it was in Connecticut. 9 in the morning. Perfect. I messaged Grandpop to ask if he could talk. When he said he could, I got to tell him all about our trip to Jerusalem. I almost said something about the magic tunnel. I knew he, of all people, would believe me. At the last second, I decided maybe I should wait until we knew more. Maybe when Grandmama and Grandpop came to visit we could take him there.

Chapter 10 - Exploring the Possibilities

In Israel, I found out, the school year always starts on September 1st. Whether it's a Sunday, a Thursday or any day except Saturday. School is six days a week, but instead of having a school day like in the US, it's a short day. At around 10, you have a break, when you eat your sandwich and a piece of fruit or something – and then at 12:45, you go home for the day and eat lunch at home. Friday, the day is even shorter and you finish at 11:45.

I found all this out the day I got my cellphone and called Gali. For her, it was just the way things were. For me, it seemed like going to school for a half day, like I did in kindergarten. I wondered what it would be like to eat lunch at home every day and have the whole afternoon free.

There were still almost four weeks until school started. I found out that the school I would be going to—the one that was right across the street from our house—was called *HaYovel*, which means *the jubilee*. They called the school that because it opened in 1998, the same year Israel celebrated its jubilee – its 50th Independence Day.

I wanted to find out more about school, but, believe me, August in Israel is hotter than anything you can imagine. Many days the temperature is over 90 degrees. In the shade. In the sun, it's unbearable. So instead of meeting Gali by the school and taking a tour to see what it looked like, we set to meet at the mall. Air conditioning was more important than I had ever realized. We went to a place where they sell funny drinks, like 'Ice cookies' – a sort of milkshake with cookie pieces. We sat there and chatted for a while, mostly in English, but Gali said a few words in Hebrew – some of which I understood and some of which I didn't. School in a different language was going to be challenging. At least math was still math, right?

I wondered if I should ask if Gali knew about the magic tunnel. Maybe all the kids knew and it was no big deal. I finally asked her what she knew about the tunnel. She explained that a few years ago the city decided that instead of graffiti they'd have people paint inside it.

"That's it?" I asked.

"Yes." She gave me a funny look, "It's just a shortcut to the park – oh, and it has a great echo!"

"Cool." I said. She had no idea. None at all. Maybe the magic had something to do with Noah and me? Maybe it was there because we needed it...

Over the next few days, Noah and I found out what classes we were going to be in – and we got to start meeting some of the kids who would be in our classes. The whole language thing was really worrying me, but the principal promised me, as she took us on a tour of the school, that I'd get as much help as I needed. She told me that lots of kids start school there not knowing Hebrew and that the school has a plenty of experience with it. I also found out that there were a few other kids in my grade level who speak English. That would help.

Every chance we got, Noah and I headed to the tunnel. Once, I tried to get into the magic rooms by myself, but it didn't work. Strangely, it only worked when I was with Noah or with Noah and Elise.

By the time we'd been in Israel for a week, Noah was starting to get really good at flips and cartwheels – both in the orange sparkly room and in the park. Of course, in the orange room, he was incredible and in the park he was just good, but still – it was hard to grasp how much he'd learned so quickly. My singing was improving too. One day, I was singing along with the radio, when my mom popped into my room surprised and asked, "Where'd you learn to sing like that?"

We took Elise with us every day, sometimes twice a day. At first, I practiced bye-bye with her. After a few times, even outside of the tunnel, she would wave with me – not like I did, but enough to see that she was moving her hand on purpose. I felt like if she could do that, she could do anything. I really, really, more-than-anything, wanted Elise to be able to talk.

Even one or two words would make a huge difference. That was what I had been focusing on once she seemed to get the hang of waving.

My mom was already used to the fact that we would take Elise and she had a bunch of 10 Shekel coins in a mug by the door that we could take any time we went out. She said that because it was so hot, it was important to drink enough. 10 Shekel was enough to get a popsicle or a slush for all three of us. Even Elise seemed to be used to the fact that we were going out.

We rushed to the tunnel, held hands, anticipating the orange sparkles and I saw Elise close her eyes. Magically, it always seemed to work. We were in the orange room. Elise was able to do bye-bye right away!

I knelt beside Elise and told her again, like I had almost every day over the past two weeks, "We're going to practice talking today." I knew it was a huge challenge and that it might never work, but I had to try.

"Say dada." I said, feeling silly, like I always did. "Dadadadada."

Nothing. Maybe that wasn't a good sound.

"OK, say baba." I tried, feeling equally silly. "Babababababa." I sounded like a sheep. I repeated it a few times. I pressed Elise's lips together, showing her how to make the sound. She seemed to be trying, but no sound came out.

"Try mama. Mamamamama." At least I didn't sound like a sheep anymore. "Mmmma. Mmmma." I wasn't really aware how I made the different sounds—how could I teach Elise? Except I thought heard just the very beginning of a 'mmm' sound. Or did I? Hard to tell...

"Elise? Mamamamama." I repeated.

"mmm" The magic was working.

Again and again I repeated it. After what felt like forever, I heard Elise say it.

"Ma" Elise looked proud of herself and I nearly fainted.

* * *

"NOAH, SHE SAID MA!" I yelled anything but calmly.

"SHE SAID MA!" I repeated, as if he didn't hear me the first time.

"Cool," was his disappointing response. He wasn't nearly as excited as I was.

My excitement quickly started to fade. I guess that's what happens when no one feels the way you do. Maybe it wasn't as big a deal as I'd thought it was. Maybe it was all in my head anyway. In any case, I was still curious to find out what the pink hallway would be—it seemed that each hallway had a different message. Convincing Noah to go there might be a problem. I tried to think of a tactic that might work.

"Noah, how about if we go to the pink today and next time you choose?" I asked carefully.

"I don't want to go into any stupid pink anything!" Noah answered just as he had the last time I'd suggested it.

"But we have to go together," I reasoned with him. "We need to be together to get out. Maybe sometime we'll come here and there will be a Ninja room and I won't want to go in." I'd clearly used the right word. Noah would do anything Ninja-related.

"OK. But if it's dumb, we're leaving right away." He said, forgetting that going into another room always seemed to work only one-way – that we would have to leave through the pink room.

"Fine." I agreed. Whatever, as long as he'd come with us.

We started walking toward the pink hallway. Like with the other colors, this time too, the hallway seemed to widen into a room and the orange room disappeared behind us. But unlike the other times, I wasn't scared.

A note fell to Noah's feet.

Here you can make a dream come true

Chapter 11 - A Dream

So far, the notes had done exactly what they said they would, so the thought that a dream of mine could come true made my heart pound. We knew what Elise's dream was – and if we knew, the magic tunnel must know too. My heart was thumping so loudly that I felt like Noah and Elise must hear it too. Noah, for a welcome change, was speechless. For the first time I understood why on TV shows, when they give a piece of really important news, they tell people to sit down. I felt as if I might faint.

A dream was huge. Maybe a once-in-a-lifetime opportunity. How would I make it count? In the back of my head, I heard, *and no wishing for more wishes...*

Instead of thinking too hard, it made sense to go ahead with something we didn't have to think about at all—Elise's dream.

"Elise wants to dance!" I spoke aloud, not sure who or what I was speaking to.

Nothing happened.

"Elise's dream is to be able to dance!" I was beginning to feel desperate. Maybe the magic was broken. Maybe that was a dream that couldn't work.

"Noah, let's get Elise up." I said.

We unbuckled her, reached for her hands, and pulled her to her feet. The feet that we knew had never carried her weight. Elise felt lighter than ever, in fact, I felt sort of weightless myself.

"Dance, Elise!" I closed my eyes, hoping something would happen.

It wasn't what I had imagined at all, but the three of us were dancing around together in a circle. Elise looked the happiest I had ever seen her. Her legs weren't doing anything, she was suspended between us as we danced in a circle, but it seemed like that was enough for her. Her smile was different from usual—more alive, more connected to what was happening.

I told Noah I wanted to twirl her around, and I did. My little ballerina sister. Wow.

With her being so light, I held her up against me and gave her a long hug. "I love you, Elise. That was a great dance!"

I couldn't think of a dream that I wanted to make come true. Maybe it was just that I was so overcome with emotion – or maybe in some ways my dream already had come true.

Noah, on the other hand, wanted to be a Ninja. While doing some of the moves he'd been practicing, his clothes turned black and Ninja-like and he started doing more sophisticated moves. I was hoping Noah's imaginary Ninja Star – OK, 'Shuriken', like Noah had made sure to tell me a billion times— would stay imaginary, otherwise this could get dangerous.

Carefully, I put Elise back into her stroller. "You're the best sister ever!" I told her.

Noah kept up his Ninja antics for a while and we wondered what to do about his costume and mask when we were ready to go, but when we pushed on the wall together to leave the tunnel, they disappeared as if they'd never existed.

After the colored-slush, we walked slowly through the park, watching the kids play. I felt like they were so different from me. They spoke a different language and were worried about different things. They were used to living in tiny apartments with hard stone floors. They probably knew nothing about magic. Was I ever going to fit in? Did I even want to fit in? How long were we going to stay in Israel?

Noah nearly bumped into someone with Elise's stroller. I apologized and we kept walking. When we got to the big wooden structure, Noah wanted to play. Since someone had to stay with Elise, I looked for a free bench, but since there wasn't one available, I ended up sitting on a stone wall off to the side.

"Want to practice bye-bye?" I asked Elise, knowing she couldn't answer. I looked at her, ready to start showing her how to do bye-bye so she could copy me.

Elise moved both her hands.

"Elise! You moved your hands!" I nearly yelled. "You know how to do it!" This time, anyone could see it was real.

"Noah!" I called him using my loudest playground voice.

He came over running, with his brown hair wet from sweat.

"What?" he answered impatiently.

"We have to go home. Elise can wave. We have to show mom!" I had to make him understand that it was important.

"She's going to be able to wave in another 10 minutes too. I'm playing with some kids over there." He pointed toward the blue slide.

"No, now!" I said insistently.

"Just 5 minutes then." Noah bargained.

I was going to have to wait another five minutes until we could leave the park and then another 7 or 8 minutes until we got home. I might explode.

Chapter 12 - Seeing is Believing

The elevator couldn't go up fast enough for me. I needed to get home and show my mom what Elise could do and see what she would say.

I kept pressing the '2' button as if that would make the elevator go up faster or at least tell the elevator how urgently we needed to get to the second floor.

We took Elise out of the elevator. New magnets seemed to appear on our front door every day. We opened the door and burst in. "MOM!" I yelled.

It didn't occur to me that yelling like that might scare her. She came running and when she saw we were all OK, she said, "Ohmigosh, you nearly gave me a heart attack! What happened?!?"

"Mom! Elise can wave bye-bye!" I said excitedly.

My mom looked doubtful.

"No, really! Show her, Elise. Show Mom bye-bye!" I pleaded.

My heart pounded. I had to see her do it again. See her do it for our mom.

Elise's hands opened and closed.

"Wow, WOW!" My mom screamed. "I have to call Dad!"

My mom called my dad and my dad told her he was going to get on the next train home. This was something he had to see.

I got my tablet and made a video of Elise moving her hands. I had to make sure I would have it on record. Then I emailed it to my grandparents.

My dad was just as happy as my mom had been when he saw Elise move her hands. It was the first time that we could know for sure that she understood something that we said. My parents were throwing around ideas about how it could have happened. Elise had had one treatment in Tel Aviv, but that wasn't the first time she'd had that type of treatment.

Nonchalantly, Noah said, "Maybe it's magic..."

I could tell my cheeks were bright red. No one else noticed.

My mom laughed and said, "Maybe Israel is just really good for Elise."

"Do you think it means she might be able to do other things?" I asked.

"We hope so, Megan." My dad said patting my head. "Just don't get your hopes up."

Too late. I thought. My hopes were so high they were way up in the sky. Then again, earlier that day I'd danced with my sister. I had good reason for hope.

It troubled me that I couldn't figure out what my dream was. Did I not have any dreams of my own? Wait. Ever since I'd heard about it, I'd wanted to see the Eiffel Tower. Could the magic tunnel get me to Paris?

My mom made macaroni and cheese for dinner that night and we ate salad. The food in Israel is so different. Even the bread is different. The bread itself is brownish and you can buy a loaf and use a bread slicer in the supermarket, which slices the whole loaf at once! My dad said it's cheaper. I say it's more fun.

The food was OK, but not like back home. I missed my old room. I missed my friends. I hated that it was so hot outside. If not for the magic tunnel, I realized, I might be completely miserable.

After dinner, my mom said she had a surprise for us. There was a tiny room in our apartment, even smaller than our bedroom, that my mom said is called a safe room. It has a thick metal door and a funny window. Apparently, if there is an air raid, you have to go into that room and close the door. My mom said that we didn't need to worry, that there wouldn't be any air raids. I wasn't worried. I had no idea what an air raid was anyway.

Later I found out that an air raid means that rockets are being launched in your direction. Definitely sounded scary. Why would anyone launch rockets at houses?

Anyway, inside the safe room, my parents had put up a big TV and there were some big beanbags for us to sit on – our own TV room. The TV was connected to cable and there were lots of channels – even things we recognized from home. Some of the cartoons were dubbed. That means that they replace the original sound with voices in another language. All the 'real people' shows that we knew were in English, with Hebrew subtitles. My mom explained that they have to dub the shows for little kids, because they can't read yet – but for older kids, they leave the original language and use subtitles. I was surprised that I was able to read and understand some of the words, even though they flashed on the screen pretty quickly.

Chapter 13 - Paris, Here I Come!

I had messaged Gali a few times and she said she wanted to invite me over to meet some more girls. My mom thought it was a good idea. She drew a little map for me and sent me out to find Gali's house. I was sure I would get lost and never find the way back home. I was imagining the search party coming to find me, only to discover I was dehydrated, sitting under a tree to catch some shade. But I followed the map and found her apartment pretty easily.

I don't like knocking on a stranger's door. Gali wasn't exactly a stranger, but I didn't know if she would be the one to open the door. I hesitated for about two minutes before I could finally bring myself to knock. The door opened quickly, but it was Gali's older brother, Danny, who opened it and then pretty much ignored me as I walked into the living room where Gali and her friends were chatting loudly.

"This is Tali," Gali said, pointing to a tall girl with long black hair pulled back in a ponytail. "This is Yael." Yael had a long brown braid and was wearing a pink tank top and jeans shorts. Yael looked to me like she could be Gali's twin, except that instead of brown eyes, hers were green. At least my long hair fit right in...

Yael and Gali both spoke English, but Tali only knew a few words. Yael translated so that we could talk. It was cool that she knew both Hebrew and English so well that she spoke both easily. Maybe I could do that someday. They told me all about school and how their teacher was sometimes late in the morning and only came in after the bell; that recess was their favorite part of the day; that this year they were separating the boys and girls for gym class.

They asked me what *khugim* I was going to do. It sounds like KHOO-GEEM, with the stress on the second syllable. I had no idea what they were talking about.

"A *khug* is a something you do after school – some are once a week and some twice – you do something you want to learn, or something that's fun. A lot of the boys go to soccer. The girls mostly go to art or gymnastics or sugar dough." Gali said.

"Sugar dough?" I wondered.

"You learn how to make decorations for cakes. I did it last year." Yael smiled. "When you're finished, you get to eat it too. That was the best part."

There was something so normal about being with the girls that I almost forgot that I was in Israel. I was a little sad that I wasn't going to be in their class, but I hoped I would see them at recess and that the girls in my class would be as nice as they were.

Gali's mom ordered pizza and everyone stayed for lunch. It seemed like it was obvious and no big deal. My mom hadn't said I could stay for lunch, so I called her first to make sure it was OK. She talked to Dena and then to me and told me it was fine. Dena poured us each a glass of a grape-flavored drink called *petel*. *Petel* actually means raspberry, but for some reason that's what they call every drink made by mixing syrup and water – no matter what flavor it is.

When it was time to go, I was pretty sure I'd manage to find my way home. Tali walked with me to the corner of the street and then waved and said, *yalla bye*, which I guess meant bye.

Two to four in the afternoon are 'quiet hours' – you can't play loud instruments, hammer nails into the wall, or even play outside. Everyone just seems to know that you can't make noise between two and four. My mom said that in the summer it doesn't really matter, since until four the sun is at its most dangerous, so it's better not to be outside anyway.

At four we had a snack and then Noah and I got ready to take Elise to the magic tunnel. My mom said that we seemed to have so much fun that maybe she should come along.

Hold on. Wait. What do I do now? Oh no… "Nah, you should finish that book you're reading. Come with us some other day." I tried to sound natural.

"OK. You're right. I'll stay in the air conditioning." My mom said.

Phew. That was a big relief. We'd never be able to go to the magic tunnel with my mom. Or could we? That would be weird. I couldn't picture it.

Since I knew what my dream was, I was going to see if the magic could make it come true. But first, in the orange room, I wanted to try to get Elise to talk some more.

Jungle boy was off flipping and twirling like a little monkey about two seconds after we got into the orange room. I asked Elise, "Do you remember how to say 'ma'?"

"Mamamamamama." I tried.

At first, nothing and then, after a few times "mmm".

I wasn't going to give up. I had to hear her say it again.

"Mamamamama, Elise." I urged her to say it too. I sent her my most powerful thought-waves. Maybe that would work.

"Mmmmmmma!" Elise had done it!

"Noah! Did you hear?" I asked excitedly. "Did you hear Elise say 'ma'?"

"Uh uh..." Noah hadn't heard. OK. She would just have to say it again.

"Elise, again, mmmmmma." I said.

Noah stood watching and I felt so proud. I crossed my fingers and hoped she would do it.

"Ma!" Elise said.

"Yay, Elise!" Noah said, and we both clapped our hands for her. Elise smiled. I was so happy that Noah had heard too—and that he was excited this time!

I couldn't wait to try getting Elise to say more, but the need to try to make my dream come true was eating at me.

I dragged Noah to the pink hallway. Monkey boy turned into Ninja boy so quickly that I felt like I would never be able to keep up with his pace. I guess the magic room remembered Noah.

"I want to see the Eiffel Tower." I said. "In Paris." How was I supposed to let the magic know what I wanted? I used my fingers to make a shape of the Eiffel Tower. I half-expected to see a paper fly down saying, 'Dream on' or 'You're out of luck this time'. But nothing happened. Nothing at all.

"My dream is to go to Paris. To eat baguettes. To wear a beret and watch a ballet." I figured throwing in every French reference I could think of might help. Nothing.

So much for my dream coming true.

"Say bye-bye to the magic tunnel, Elise." I said, disappointed. Elise waved. How could I be disappointed when magical things were happening? "Say bye-bye to Megan's dream of going to Paris." Elise waved again. She didn't get it.

Chapter 14 - Never Give Up

I walked home glum. I tried to think that I hadn't really expected to see the Eiffel Tower and that even magic has to have its limits. Definitely a shame, but I probably should have expected it. What had I even been thinking to wish that? We walked slowly and I managed to mumble 'yeah' or 'no' as Noah-the-chatterbox asked me all sorts of questions. I tried to cheer myself up in the elevator, so my mom wouldn't ask me what was wrong. I thought about my new school and how much fun it would be to finish early. I thought about how cool it would be, when we moved back to the US, to tell people I had lived in Israel...

My mom was waiting with dinner ready when we got home. Chicken and rice. It smelled so good and tasted even better. I have to say – the rice in Israel tastes completely different. It makes the rice back in the States seem bland. This rice was amazing, especially with gravy from the chicken.

My dad was home kind of early, which was strange, since it was Tuesday – and Tuesday was the day that he usually had the most meetings. He talked to us about what work was like and said things were going pretty much like he expected. He asked us what we were up to. 'Nothing much' was the best I could come up with. Noah said he wanted to do gymnastics – that he was getting really good at cartwheels and flips.

After dinner, my dad went to the park with Noah and me and Noah showed him a handstand—even I didn't know he could do that. He also did some pretty amazing cartwheels. My dad said that it looked like he had a lot of potential and that he really should do gymnastics.

"You can sign him up for a *khug*," I said.

"A what?" My dad looked at me as if he was about to start laughing.

"It's an afterschool program that you go to every week at the same time. Gali told me about them – she said there are a million to choose from – chess, art, soccer…" I explained, feeling very knowledgeable.

"Well, a gymnastics HOOG it is!" My dad said, sounding silly.

As we walked back home, we passed through the magic tunnel. Noah and I looked and smiled at each other and walked right through. Nothing suspicious. Maybe because we were holding my dad's hands?

We sat down at the kitchen table for a drink of water and my dad told my mom how fabulous Noah's handstands and cartwheels were. My mom said, "This, I've got to see..." and Noah went and did a handstand in the living room, which I thought was a terrible idea – he could crash into stuff. My mom was impressed. Secretly, I was too.

My mom said she was taking Elise for her bath and my dad asked her to wait a second – he had something to tell us. My mom already knew, but my dad must have wanted her to be there.

"Like I told you earlier, things are going well at work and, I didn't think I would have to travel much – or so soon..." My dad began.

I braced myself, because I knew this meant that my dad was going to have to go to the US for a while and

I was going to miss him terribly. It wasn't fair, because we had been in Israel for just a few weeks and he was already going back. I felt myself getting angry.

"I came home early today because it turns out that I have to fly out tomorrow morning for a few meetings." He continued.

Shoot. I was right. I felt the tears coming into my eyes. I really didn't want my dad to go away.

"Anyway, it's just for a few days and it's only to France."

My ears suddenly felt pointy, like those of a cat. They were in full-hearing mode.

"So…" my dad went on, "Since the school year hasn't started yet and I just have two short meetings there…"

Wait. What did this have to do with the school year?

"And Megan's always wanted to go to Paris." my mom put in.

My dad could not talk fast enough.

"I bought a ticket for Megan too. Megan, get packed up – we're flying to Paris in the morning!"

My mom was standing there next to Elise, with tears streaming down her face. I was waiting for my dad to yell 'April Fool's' but it was August and my dad wouldn't do that to me. At least I hoped he wouldn't.

"Really???" I said.

"Really." My mom said. "When dad suggested it, I thought it was a great idea. Noah – some other time it will be your turn." My mom said.

"Wow!" I turned to Elise, who suddenly looked sad. I didn't recall ever seeing her look sad before.

"Elise. Don't worry, I'm only going to be gone for a little while and you'll stay here with Noah and mom."

Everyone was looking at Elise, which made it even more special when we all heard her say her very first word, "Ma".

...

I looked at my parents. They were beaming. Elise was too. Even Noah smiled a big smile. Secretly, I wondered if Elise's first word was a gift from the magic tunnel. Did it matter? For now, I was just going to be happy and focus on packing. Next up, Paris! I couldn't wait.

Special thanks to Romi Sussman who read an earlier version and hopefully spared me no criticism! Thank you also to Bethami Gold, Leah Goodman, Rona Michelson, and Carol Donohue McIntosh (and her sons) who patiently read chapter-by-chapter as I wrote.

Thank you to my son, Yirmi, who wrote all the magic messages!

Thank you to my husband, Ohad, who helps and encourages me to make my dreams come true. I hope I always do the same for you ♥

And one last **thank you** to my Savta Leah (Lena), who left behind a hidden treasure—a story she published in 1926 in a literary journal at Radcliffe. Finding it just as I was about to publish my own book really was magical.